Legend says that Black Rock
is the home of a Wicked Witch.

Over the years she has lured
many sailors to their doom.

Who will be the Witch's next victim?

other books by Horace Dobbs

CAMERA UNDERWATER

UNDERWATER SWIMMING

SNORKELLING AND SKINDIVING
AN INTRODUCTION

FOLLOW A WILD DOLPHIN

SAVE THE DOLPHINS

DOLPHIN SPOTTER'S HANDBOOK

THE MAGIC OF DOLPHINS

THE GREAT DIVING ADVENTURE

CLASSIC DIVES OF THE WORLD

TALE OF TWO DOLPHINS

DANCE TO A DOLPHIN'S SONG

JOURNEY INTO DOLPHIN DREAMTIME

Dilo and the Call of the Deep

Dilo makes Friends

Dilo and the Treasure Hunters

Horace Dobbs

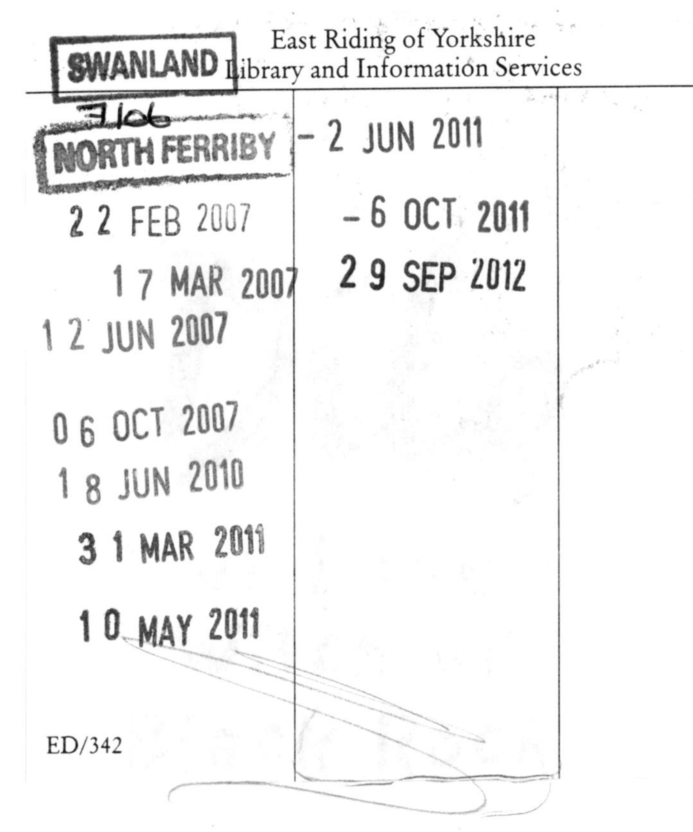

Illustrated by Rico

Watch Publishing
'Dolphin'
10 Melton Road
North Ferriby
East Yorkshire
HU14 3ET
England
Tel: 01482 632650
Fax: 01482 634914
Email: idw@talk21.com
Website: www.idw.org

ISBN
0-9541721-1-6

Printed by
Redcliff Print & Design
30 The Weir
Hessle
East Yorkshire
HU13 0RU
Tel: 01482 640428
Fax: 01482 641390

Contents

Chapter	Title	Page
1	"We're free!"	7
2	Chance of a lifetime	14
3	Summer holidays	19
4	The return of Sea Wolf	24
5	The witch and the mermaid	31
6	Debra's nightmare	35
7	Into the net	40
8	Mission accomplished	47
9	Beth and Ann	52
10	Bulletin Board	59
11	Daisy	65
12	What kind of place is this?	72
13	Come on Daisy	76
14	Star	81
15	Postie's plan	84
16	A slippery customer	89
17	Detective work	93
18	Fearsome Fivesome	99
19	A ray of hope	103
20	Unexpected help	105
21	Going home	111
22	The Daisy appeal	117
23	Moving with the times	120
24	Daisy disappears	122

This book is dedicated to Chloe
who lives in the little fishing
village of Polperro in Cornwall
where dolphins sometimes
come to play.

1

"We're Free"

The sun was sinking slowly towards the sea when Debra climbed down the rough steps from the lighthouse to the sea below. It was a calm, mild evening. The wind had dropped completely. The sea gently slurped against the rocks.

Debra put on her mask, fins and snorkel. She slipped into the water and swam down to the seabed. Her ears popped. Debra picked up two stones and clapped them together. Then, still holding the stones, she kicked with her fins and soared upwards. Debra surfaced well away from the cliff path. Above her she could see the lighthouse. Leaning on the wall was her twin brother, Robin. Uncle Pat was standing beside him. Debra waved to them and they both waved back.

"That twin sister of yours is just like a fish," said Pat.

Dilo the dolphin was chasing a flat fish across the sand when he heard the sound of Debra cracking stones together. In an instant he turned. With his tail pumping up and down at full speed, he headed towards the lighthouse steps. Although he couldn't see Debra with his eyes his sonar detected her. He recognised the picture the reflected sound created in his mind. It was his favourite human friend.

Dilo stayed submerged, skimming at full speed just above the sea bed. As he approached the cliff Dilo turned upwards. Now he could see Debra with his eyes. She was treading water. He raced towards her. A second later he burst through the surface.

Dilo's sonar, which he called his Magic Sound, sounded like a squeak to Debra. When she heard it she knew he was on his way. Debra was so excited, she felt as if her body was full of tiny popping bubbles. Even so, she did not expect Dilo to arrive so quickly. When the dolphin rocketed out of the water bedside her she shrieked with surprise and delight.

"Dilo!" she screamed at the top of her voice as the dolphin flew high into the air.

Debra looked up as Dilo curved over her head. The sinking sun was gleaming on the water falling from his body. For a speck of time Dilo hung over Debra. She saw the star on his glistening dorsal fin as Dilo nosed down into the sea.

Before Debra had recovered from the shock, Dilo turned underwater and was once again flying over her head. Looking up Debra saw the dolphin's smooth round belly soaring above her. Debra was so excited, she felt as if she too was high in the sky with Dilo. Their two spirits were one. They were both free. Free to fly in the sky. Free to dive into the sea. Free to explore the magic depths of the ocean. When Dilo speared out of the water for the third time Debra held both arms aloft as high as she could.

"Yippee! We're free! We're free!" she shouted at the top of her voice.

After his third jump Dilo slowed down. He swam in a circle around Debra. Debra watched as the dolphin's dorsal fin sliced through the surface towards her. Dilo's invitation was obvious. Debra clasped her hands around the dolphin's fin. She inhaled deeply as she was tugged through the water. The next instant Debra was beneath the surface. Dilo was taking her into his realm. The colours changed as she was pulled downwards into a world of luminous blue.

Fronds of kelp, growing like miniature trees from the dark rocks, swayed out of the way as they passed by. Little fishes, like silver needles, darted for cover. Her arms outstretched, her legs trailing, and her long hair billowing like the mane of a galloping horse, Debra flew through a canyon.

Suddenly it got darker. They were gliding under an overhang of rock. There were no seaweeds now. Debra was in another kingdom. Crabs lurked in crevices. A lobster waved its long feelers as Debra glided past. Sea anemones, like flowers, grew out of the rocks amidst sponges and starfish. Every surface was adorned with spirals and circles of tiny feathery petals. Debra felt as if she was in a dream, flying through a jewel box.

Debra's magical journey took her down to where the rocks met the sand. Stretching before her, as far as she could see, was a desert. Above it the sea disappeared into a pale blue mist. Dilo turned. Rocks reappeared. She was moving up towards the light. Dilo rose quickly. Soon they were over the kelp. From underneath the sea Debra saw the sun dancing on the surface. Just when she felt she could hold her breath no longer, Debra passed out of Dilo's world back into her own.

Debra gulped some air and released her grip. Dilo's fin slid away from her. It dipped beneath the surface and was gone. The dolphin had left to catch his supper. Moments later Debra saw a flash as Dilo tossed a fish into the air.

Debra was filled with happiness as she swam back to the lighthouse steps. It was the first day of the holiday and she had made contact with her beloved dolphin.

2

Chance of a lifetime

Dilo the dolphin liked people. In fact he liked them so much he spent most of his time in a bay where there were lots of people and lots of boats. He enjoyed nothing more than to ride the bow waves of fishing boats full of holiday-makers and then jump as high as he could into the sky.

Sometimes he deliberately landed with a huge splash. This would send spray flying. The fishermen knew what to expect and would duck out of the way. The unsuspecting passengers would shriek with surprise when they were drenched with sea water. Their cries would soon turn to laughter when they got over the shock.

In fact that was the main reason why most of them were on the boats. They had seen the sign on the jetty: TRIPS TO SEE THE DOLPHIN and decided it might be a pleasant way to spend some time. If they were undecided and wandered off, a man, who looked like a fisherman, would approach. Actually he wasn't a fisherman at all. He was an out-of-work actor who helped the fishermen find customers.

"Don't miss the chance of a lifetime," he would say. "See the dolphin in his natural environment - children half price."

If they moved on he would walk alongside

them telling them what a wonderful experience it would be.

"You'll be sorry you missed this wonderful opportunity," he would continue. "The dolphin could be gone tomorrow. You'll regret it if you miss out."

If this line was successful he would steer the group towards the steps on the jetty. Then, in a loud triumphant voice, he would shout to the boatman, “Four more for a trip to see the dolphin, Boss.”

He called the fishermen ‘Boss’. It made them feel important. He also made sure that they knew it was him who had enticed their passengers on board. In that way the boatmen wouldn’t mind quite so much giving him a share of their takings.

He enjoyed acting the part of the barker and was always on the lookout, even when he was helping customers onto the boat. If he saw any likely trippers on the jetty he would call up to them. “This way ladies and gentlemen for a boat trip around the bay. See the dolphin.” Then he would add, “The boat leaves shortly.”

What he really meant was the boat would leave as soon as it was full. How long that was depended on his touting skills.

Most of those who went out to see the dolphin were holiday-makers who had wandered onto the jetty. Sprinkled amongst them, however, were others who had travelled long distances to see Dilo. They felt especially attracted to dolphins.

For them a visit to Lighthouse Bay was a pilgrimage. To see a wild dolphin at close quarters was a dream come true.

The fishermen had their own reason for liking Dilo. He brought extra trade - lots of extra trade - for their boat trips. There was plenty of friendly rivalry with the nearest fishing port that didn't have a dolphin like Dilo to attract tourists.

Nobody knew why Dilo had chosen to stay in Lighthouse Bay. So the fishermen made up a story. They said his mother had been killed by a shark and the orphan dolphin had been fed by fishermen. "That's why he is so friendly and stays here," they reasoned.

This was partly true. For Dilo was in fact an orphan. His mother had been accidentally killed in a fishing net far away off Seal Island. After that he wandered until he swam into Lighthouse Bay. It was a safe haven and there were plenty of fish to eat. But the main reason why he stayed was because one day he met a girl swimming in the sea. They became friends. Her name was Debra.

3

Summer holidays

It was the height of the season. The village bustled with holiday makers. Throughout the day the fishing boats, loaded with passengers, left the jetty. As soon as one departed another one would pull alongside the stone steps. Business was brisk and the six little fishing boats running dolphin trips were fully occupied all day. Everyone was happy.

Because it was inside a large bay the harbour was protected. The entrance to the bay was through a deep channel between high cliffs. Outside was the mighty ocean. Right in line with the entrance to the bay was a jagged rock. It was called Black Rock. Over the centuries it had claimed many ships. Indeed, originally the bay was called Black Bay. But when a lighthouse was built on the top of the cliffs it was renamed Lighthouse Bay.

The lighthouse was painted white and pointed towards the sky like a giant finger. It was a safety marker which, for many years after it was built, helped approaching boats steer clear of the dreaded Black Rock. Now all the big fishing boats had radar and GPS (Global Positioning Satellite) navigation. They didn't need the lighthouse to steer safely into the harbour. Nonetheless they liked to see it standing boldly on top of the cliffs.

Pat, whose real name was Patrick, lived in a sturdy house alongside the lighthouse. Pat was a Warden for International Wildlife Watch. His job was to observe and record the wildlife in the area.

Pat had a variety of jobs before he became a warden. These included being a lighthouse keeper and working as a deck hand on fishing boats. But his job as warden was the one he liked most of all. He had always enjoyed watching seabirds. Over the years, without knowing it, he had become quite an expert. Now he could watch the birds and get paid for it.

Pat was a bachelor and enjoyed his solitary life. His needs were few. He grew some of his own vegetables in a small walled garden. He caught fish off the rocks. Pat cooked on an ancient stove fuelled with driftwood.

Pat seldom left the lighthouse. Those who wanted to see him had to visit his lonely home. Pat's favourite visitor was Postie the postman, who, when necessary, brought supplies as well as letters. The lighthouse was his last delivery. Postie had given up a well-paid job in a big city to become a rural postman. He never regretted that decision. The two men would spend hours swapping stories. If the weather was good they would stand outside in the sunshine. But mostly they sat chatting with mugs of tea beside the stove in the kitchen.

The arrival of Dilo brought a new interest into their lives. It happened just before Pat's sister Mary, whom he seldom saw, was taken seriously ill. She begged her brother to look after her two children for a while. She didn't tell him that they were known locally as the "Terrible Twins" because of the mischief they got up to.

At first the middle-aged bachelor strongly resisted the idea. He certainly didn't want two children tearing around the place. He was quite happy with his dog Boka and his cat Sprat for company.

Robin and Debra's arrival, in the pouring rain, was not a happy experience for Pat. But eventually they settled in. Robin was mad about computers and brought his own with him. When he showed his uncle how it could be used to store and analyse information about wildlife, Pat became a convert. Soon the two of them were engrossed, with Robin proudly showing his uncle things he never knew were possible.

It was Dilo the dolphin though who cemented the friendship between Pat and his niece Debra. They grew to love the friendly dolphin in completely different ways and for completely different reasons. Debra enjoyed swimming with Dilo. The bond between the girl and the dolphin grew even stronger when Mike, a local diver, gave Debra a wetsuit and taught her to dive.

To Pat, Dilo was a symbol of freedom. The dolphin reminded him of his earlier years when he was a seaman and the many times he watched dolphins playing around the bow of his boat.

Robin couldn't swim and didn't like to admit that he was a bit scared of the sea. One day he slipped off the rocks and fell into the water. Fortunately Dilo was nearby and saved him from drowning. After that Robin set up a special file on his computer and recorded all Dilo's movements and activities.

Debra and Robin visited their uncle whenever they could. Now they were back for the summer holidays. It was their first day and the twins were looking forward to new adventures.

4

The return of Sea Wolf

When Debra arrived at the lighthouse the first thing she wanted to do was jump into the sea to swim with Dilo. But it was Sunday and the bay was buzzing with boats of all kinds. Debra knew most of them would leave in the early evening. So she decided to wait until then, when she hoped to have Dilo to herself - for a little while at least.

It was a glorious sunny day. After standing by the wall outside the lighthouse the twins walked to one of their favourite places on the top of the cliffs. It was in a slight hollow away from the path. From their lofty perch they could see most of the bay. In the distance was the harbour. Rows of brightly coloured houses and small hotels lined the waterfront. Behind them rose majestic hills.

Below the lighthouse was a deep channel. It led to the wide open sea that stretched to the

horizon and sparkled silver in the bright sunshine. There was just one break in the vast expanse of blue, Black Rock, a lonely outcrop of dark stone. Even on a lovely day like today it looked sinister. Black Rock was surrounded by a necklace of white foam where the waves were broken by sharp rocks.

"Uncle Pat says there's a hidden cave on Black Rock," said Debra.

"He also says it's the home of a witch," added Robin.

"Do you believe that?" asked Debra.

"I'd need scientific proof first," replied Robin.

"Oh *you* would. I wonder where Dilo is?" said Debra changing the subject.

In the distance sailing ships leaned over in the breeze. Most of the boating activity, however, was concentrated in a cove opposite the lighthouse. Small vessels of different shapes and sizes were gathering there. Debra knew why. A few moments later Dilo's dorsal fin rose briefly out of the sea and then disappeared. The dolphin was heading towards a boat packed with visitors.

When Dilo surfaced, the twins heard shrieks of delight as those on board rushed to one side. They all wanted the dolphin to come close enough to touch. Dilo obliged, letting some of the passengers briefly touch his fin. Then suddenly Dilo dived and vanished.

Those on board could not see in which direction he was heading. From their lookout on top of the cliffs Debra and her brother could. They saw the dolphin's dark shape speeding like a torpedo towards another boat in the middle of the bay.

It was a small cabin cruiser towing an inflated car tyre inner-tube. Hanging onto the tube were two people in wetsuits. In the next instant there was an explosion in the water beside them. Dilo burst through the surface. He soared into the air. For a moment he looked like a shining, silver bridge. Then he was back into the sea again. Dilo turned instantly. Three seconds later the dolphin was once again flying over the startled swimmers.

Debra couldn't stop herself. She jumped up and shrieked. "Wow, what a jump! Do it again Dilo!"

"Sit down Debbie," said her brother. "Don't make a spectacle of yourself. You've seen him do that before."

"I know," said Debra, "but every time he does it I feel so excited."

“Oh, you’re incorrigible,” said Robin.

“What does incorrigible mean?” asked Debra indignantly.

“I don’t know,” said Robin, “ but whatever it is - that’s what you are.”

“I can’t wait to go for a swim with Dilo again.”

“You said you would wait until this evening when everything has quietened down,” remembered Robin.

“I know - but it doesn’t stop me being impatient does it?”

It was then that Robin noticed a powerboat moving through the channel. He recognised it instantly.

“Look,” he called to Debra. “There’s *Sea Wolf*. I wonder what that’s doing here?”

“Probably on holiday like everyone else,” replied Debra.

“Whenever that boat’s been here in the past there’s been trouble,” continued Robin. “Come on Sis, let’s get back to the lighthouse. I want to have a look at *Sea Wolf* through the telescope.”

It was late afternoon before Debra finally got into the sea with Dilo. When the dolphin towed her down into his underwater realm, Debra expected it to be the first of many more magical swims with Dilo. But evil forces were afoot. As she climbed back out of the water Debra did not know that she would never again swim with Dilo in Lighthouse Bay that summer.

5

The Witch and the Mermaid

Debra was filled with joy after her swim with Dilo. She told Robin and Pat excitedly about it as they ate their evening meal. This got Pat into one of his talkative moods. The two children loved it when this happened.

"Have you heard the legend of Black Rock?" he asked them. "It's a rather gruesome tale."

"Oh good," said Robin, who liked horror stories.

"The legend says that Black Rock is the home of an evil spirit. It sometimes appears in the form of a woman. An old hag. She is known as the Witch of Black Rock." Pat paused for effect. "Most of the time she is quiet. When the weather is calm she stays well hidden. When there is a strong wind she moans. The legend says that the noise is the Witch of Black Rock casting a spell. If a ship's crew fall under her spell they are lured into the rocks. When the ship founders and the crew drown, the Witch of Black Rock turns them into crows. Most of the old fishermen around here are very superstitious. That's why they keep well clear of Black Rock - even when the weather is good. If they see a crow they think it's a bad omen."

"Do you think the Witch of Black Rock caused the shipwreck of the *Santa Maria*?" asked Debra.

"Well, that's what the old fishermen believe," added Pat, recalling how Debra and her diving buddy Mike came upon the wreck after it was uncovered by a wild storm.

Debra remembered the adventures she had had around Black Rock, including the day she and Dilo discovered a gold ring buried in the sand. It was inscribed with love knots and Debra had worn it every day since. It was her most treasured possession.

"Do you know there is always a balance between good and evil," continued Pat. "It's called Yin and Yang."

"Yin and Yang are strange words," said Debra.

"Well, if the Witch of Black Rock is Yin, then there has to be a Yang," continued Pat.

"What do you mean?"

"The Yang is the Mermaid of The Silent Pool."

"Oh tell us about her," pleaded Debra.

"You know there is a cleft in the cliffs opposite the lighthouse. It leads into a big pool. It is usually calm in there, even in wild weather. That's why it's called The Silent Pool."

"That's where Dilo goes when he needs to be quiet. That's where we took him when he was injured by the propeller of that awful boat *Sea Wolf*," added Debra.

"That's correct," said Pat

"We never did find out if *Sea Wolf* was running drugs did we?" piped up Robin.

"No." said Debra sharply. She didn't like

Robin interrupting. “Go on Uncle Pat, please tell us about the Mermaid,” pleaded Debra.

“Well the story goes that The Silent Pool, as it is called by the local fishermen, is the home of a mermaid who sometimes comes to the rescue of the victims of the Witch of Black Rock.”

Before the twins could ask anymore questions Pat said firmly, “It’s getting late. That’s enough for tonight. It’s time you two went to bed.”

6

Debra's nightmare

Debra didn't sleep well that night. She dreamt she was on the top of the cliffs looking down on Black Rock. It was night time. The rock opened. Flames and smoke were pouring out of a cave. Slowly a witch appeared in the inferno. Her eyes glowed like red hot coals. Dilo was swimming nearby. The witch called out, "Dilo, Dilo," in a moaning voice. The dolphin surfaced and listened. He was caught in the witch's spell and started to swim towards the rock.

Debra wanted to warn Dilo. "Keep away Dilo, keep away," she tried to shout. But no sound would come out of her mouth.

Debra panicked. She ran along a path that should have led to the sea. But the path always went the wrong way. Debra rushed this way and that. No matter how hard she tried she couldn't reach the water. All the time she could see Black

Rock and could hear the Witch laughing like a demon. She had to warn Dilo.

Then the wind started to blow. Huge waves lashed Black Rock. Lightening flashed and thunder crashed. Dilo leapt out of the raging sea. Higher and higher he rose. At the top of his jump the Witch let out a blood curdling screech.

At that moment Dilo turned into a giant crow. "Caw, caw," cried the huge black bird as it flew off into the dark night sky. The witch, wailing in triumph, slid into the sea and vanished as lightning zig-zagged across the dark sky. For a speck of time it lit the crow flying far away. A moment later there was a loud clap of thunder.

The noise woke Debra with a start. She sat up in bed. Slowly Debra realised she had been dreaming. She instinctively reached for the ring on her finger. She twisted it. Debra recalled the swim she had had with Dilo a short time ago. Touching the ring made Debra feel warm inside. The fear that had gripped her vanished.

Debra got out of bed, walked to the window and opened it. Outside the air was still.

There was no storm. All was silent. Stars shone in the sky and their reflections sparkled on the water. In the distance was Black Rock, black as coal in the dark blue sea. Debra thought she could see the silhouette of a boat close to the rock. But she wasn't sure. It didn't matter anyway. There was no lightening, no thunder and no witch.

"Thank goodness it was only a dream," Debra murmured to herself as she climbed back into bed. Soon she was fast asleep.

When Debra woke the next morning the sun was shining. She looked out of the window. The sky was blue all over. The sea was flat calm. Even Black Rock looked peaceful. It was going to be another glorious day.

On the floor beside her bed Debra saw a black feather. She bent down and picked it up.

"I hope that's not a bad omen," she said quietly to herself.

But it was.

7

Into the net

Dilo continued to fish after he left Debra. When darkness fell the dolphin moved towards the entrance to the bay. The tide was turning. Water was beginning to stream through the channel beneath the lighthouse, carrying with it small fishes. With them came the salmon.

It had been a busy day for Dilo. He was hungry. Dilo scanned the sea with his magic sound, or sonar. Then came the signal he was waiting for.

Dilo focused his sonar on a salmon and fixed its position precisely. He surfaced, snatched a quick breath, and then sped towards his prey at top speed. The fish sensed Dilo's sonar and raced for cover. The dolphin changed course. Like a missile Dilo homed in on the salmon as it darted towards Black Rock.

Dilo was on course. As he closed in the

dolphin fired the loudest sound beam he could. The salmon was stunned. A second later Dilo's jaws clamped on his unlucky prey. Without stopping Dilo headed up towards the surface. Like a footballer scoring a winning goal, he tossed his prize high into the air and caught it in his mouth.

It was the signal those on board *Sea Wolf* had been looking for. They were cruising slowly near Black Rock, sweeping the sea with a powerful torch. They were looking for Dilo. The second time Dilo tossed the salmon it flashed briefly in the beam. They had found what they were looking for.

The crew on *Sea Wolf* sprang into action immediately. They had a device which they felt sure would lure the dolphin. It was an underwater scooter. When a diver held onto the handles he was pulled through the water and could steer it in any direction.

"Lower the net," barked the man who was in charge of the operation. His order was obeyed.

Sea Wolf moved slowly forward. The weighted net hung down in the water in a Ushaped tunnel between two wooden poles. It was a dolphin trap.

"Go with the scooter," came the next order.

A man in a black wetsuit and wearing fins, mask and snorkel jumped overboard holding the scooter. He hit the sea with a splash. He switched on the motor and turned on the light. The scooter pulled him along the surface. Then, taking a deep breath, he directed the scooter downwards.

The man in charge watched the shadowy figure moving under the water. His trap was set, and just as he hoped, Dilo was heading towards *Sea Wolf*. The noise of the net going overboard had attracted the dolphin. As soon as the man with the scooter dived, Dilo rushed to investigate. The diver with the scooter did a barrel roll and then turned around sharply. Dilo had never seen a swimmer so agile before. This was a new game. When the man twisted and twirled Dilo got more and more excited. He mimicked the diver who stayed close alongside *Sea Wolf* and rose to the surface to take breaths between dives.

"Take the dolphin round to the net, " roared

the man on the deck.

The diver stayed on the surface and steered towards the net. Dilo followed the man's fins.

"He's behind you," roared the man on the deck. Dilo was over the net.

"Stop!" yelled the man to the diver. "We've got him. Haul in the net," he yelled to the two crewmen.

The diver turned sharply. The light from the scooter shone into Dilo's face. Dilo tried to twist round but he couldn't. The net stopped him. Dilo was trapped. He didn't struggle.

The men winched Dilo up out of the sea. They swung the davit and lowered the dolphin into a cradle on the deck. Dilo's flippers were slipped into the holes specially for that purpose.

The entire operation had gone without a hitch. It relied upon Dilo being friendly and curious. Being true to his nature, the dolphin had done exactly what his captors hoped he would.

When he was safely suspended in the cradle Dilo heard the twin engines throb into full power. With spray flying from the bow *Sea Wolf* sped out of Lighthouse Bay, far away from the place where Dilo had swum with Debra just a few hours earlier.

8

Mission accomplished

During the night Dilo was watched over by the man who had lured him into the net.

"Don't you die on me you great fish," he said.

Dilo liked the sound of the man's voice and gasped heavily through his blowhole.

When the sun rose another man came on deck. The boat slowed. An awning was put over Dilo to keep off the sun. The man kept Dilo sprayed with water as the boat progressed at a slow speed throughout the day. In the late afternoon *Sea Wolf* cruised to a stop. Dilo heard the anchor chain rattle over the side. The engines revved and finally stopped.

As the sun set the diver who had caught Dilo came back on deck. Dilo felt forlorn. The dolphin tried to communicate with the man. He wanted to tell him that he wasn't angry, just sad at what had been done. The man removed the awning and Dilo could see the stars. The dolphin remembered how, when he went to the surface of the sea on the night his mother died, he saw her outline in the stars. It confirmed something he felt deep inside. He knew her spirit would always be there. The sight of the stars comforted the lonely dolphin. Then, as now, he could feel his mother's presence. There were other dolphins with her. They were swimming in the night sky. The heaviness Dilo had been feeling started to disappear. Dilo felt light.

"I'm coming to join you," said Dilo as he started to float out of the cradle.

"Come on dolphin, breathe, breathe," came an urgent voice from far away.

"Don't peg out on me now."

The man was speaking to Dilo. He stroked Dilo's head. Dilo took a long breath and once again was aware of his weight.

"Phew, thank goodness for that," said the man with relief. "You haven't breathed for so long I thought you'd gone."

Shortly after that all of the crew were on deck.

"It's nearly high water," said the man in charge. "I'm going to get as close inshore as I can."

All lights on the boat were switched off. The engines started and the black-hulled boat slid slowly towards the beach.

"That's as far as I can go. We're just touching the bottom," said the man at the wheel.

The winch motor hummed as Dilo was lifted out of the boat. Four crewmen jumped into the sea, which came up to their chests. Each one took the end of a pole as Dilo was lowered into the water.

Dilo felt great relief to be back in the sea again. He breathed deeply for the first time since his capture. His pectoral fins were still sticking through the holes in the canvas stretcher. The men were holding it so he couldn't move. They steadied themselves in the water.

"You three OK?" asked the head diver in a husky voice.

"Yeah," his companions answered.

"Come on then, let's finish the job," he continued.

They floated Dilo almost to the shore.

"Now comes the tricky bit," said the leader.

"Turn him sideways and pull out the poles."

The men waited for a small wave to carry Dilo forward. Then they removed the poles and quickly pulled the canvas from under the dolphin. When the next wave came they pushed Dilo as far as they could up the beach. When it receded Dilo felt gritty sand rubbing into his skin. The dolphin thrashed his tail but it waved in the air.

"We'll have to wait to make sure a wave doesn't lift him free."

When the next big wave came and lifted Dilo briefly off the sand, the men pushed Dilo higher up the beach. After that none of the waves reached the dolphin. The tide had turned. Dilo would never get away now.

"Let's go back to the boat," said the chief diver. He took one last look at Dilo.

"Good luck dolphin," he said as he waded back into the sea.

Sea Wolf had moved out into slightly deeper water. The men swam the last part of the journey, taking the poles and the canvas sling with them. They were all back on board when the man in charge came out of the wheelhouse. He was holding a phone to his ear.

"Mission accomplished, the dolphin's in position on the beach. Now it's up to you," he said as he stepped back into the wheelhouse.

It was beginning to get light. The engines roared and *Sea Wolf* sped towards the open sea, leaving Dilo stranded on the empty beach.

9

Beth and Ann

As the sun rose, the seaside town of Crookhaven stirred into life. A few early morning risers jogged along the promenade. The tide was well out. The barnacle-encrusted legs of the pier stood like tree trunks on the wet, yellow sand.

Beth and Ann, two sisters, lived close to the pier with their parents and a golden retriever called Scamper - or Scamp for short - a dog of boundless energy.

"Why don't you girls take Scamp for a walk on the beach while I'm getting breakfast ready?" said their mother when the two girls appeared in the kitchen.

The mention of the word 'walk' sent Scamp rushing around the room, her tail thumping into the cupboards.

A few moments later the girls were out of the house and running towards the steps that led down to the beach, with Scamp bounding at their heels. On the sand they found a stick and threw it towards the water. Scamp raced after it and picked it up. When Beth tried to take it away from her, the dog darted away with it still between her teeth. When both girls pretended to ignore Scamp, she dropped the stick at their feet, pleading with sad eyes for one of them to throw it again.

Ann threw the stick. Scamp raced after it but didn't stop when she reached it. Instead the dog rushed on past the stick and started to bark wildly, jumping up and down as if she had springs on her feet. Scamp was rushing around what looked at first sight to be a log on the sand. The girls ran towards the excited dog.

Scamp had found Dilo.

When the girls arrived Dilo took a breath. It sounded like a snort.

"It's a dolphin," said Beth hardly able to believe her eyes. "What can we do?"

"We must get it back into the sea as soon as possible," replied Ann. "We need help."

Although the girls didn't know it, help of a

kind was on hand. Ever since Dilo had been put on the beach a man with binoculars had been watching the dolphin. Two girls and a dog. It couldn't be better.

When the girls saw the man walking towards them Beth rushed up to him.

"We've found a stranded dolphin," she blurted out. "Will you help us put it back in the sea?"

The man was very friendly and hurried forward to look at Dilo. He knew what to do.

"We must make sure it doesn't get too hot. We must find some way of keeping it cool." he said.

The man walked round Dilo and looked at the dolphin carefully.

"It doesn't look in very good condition does it?" he said, with a serious look on his face. "The best place for this dolphin is in the aquarium. It'll get expert attention there."

"Don't you think it would be better off back in the sea?" asked Beth.

"I don't think so," said the man looking

even more serious. "Tell you what, why don't I phone the aquarium. You two can stay and keep an eye on it while I get help."

The man took a mobile phone out of his pocket and punched in some numbers as he walked off up the beach. He was out of earshot when he spoke. The person who answered had been waiting for the call.

"Two girls and a dog have discovered the dolphin. Get down here right away. They want to put the dolphin back in the sea but I've told them it needs special care. I've already got a reporter and a photographer lined up. I'll call them. Then I'll come back to the aquarium. I need to stay well clear of the scene. I don't want anyone to know I've been involved. Get going straight away before anyone else turns up. Everything has gone exactly to plan so far."

Five minutes later a van from Crookhaven Aquarium drove across the sands towards Dilo. Everyone knew exactly what they had to do.

Then a car with a photographer and a reporter arrived. The photographer took some pictures of Beth and Ann looking at Dilo. He posed them to make a good picture and even managed to include Scamp who was scampering around with excitement. Within a few minutes the team from the aquarium had rolled Dilo onto a stretcher and lifted the dolphin into the back of the van.

As the van sped off the reporter asked the girls for details of their age, what they were doing on the beach, and how they had discovered the dolphin. He scribbled notes in pencil onto a pad, flipped it shut, thanked the girls for their help and then drove off with the photographer.

Beth, Ann and Scamp ran all the way back home to tell of their adventure.

That evening Beth and Ann saw their pictures in the local newspaper under the bold headline: DOLPHIN SAVED. Underneath, it reported how the two girls had found the dolphin on the beach in the early morning. There was no mention of the man who had appeared on the scene. The paragraph finished with, "The girls summoned help from the Crookhaven Aquarium".

It was followed by a quote from the Curator of the Aquarium: "The prompt action of these two girls undoubtedly saved the life of this dolphin, which was in poor condition. However, I am pleased to report it is making a good recovery in our pool. It is already becoming friendly with Daisy our performing dolphin. All dolphins love to play the clown. It is lucky to be alive. Perhaps it will join our dolphin show when it has fully recovered."

10
Bulletin Board

The first thing Debra wanted to do the morning after her nightmare was to make sure Dilo was safe and well. The weather was perfect.

"I'm going for a swim with Dilo before breakfast," she announced cheerfully to her uncle who was busying himself in the kitchen.

"Off you go then," said Pat with a smile "I won't start cooking until you get back".

Debra bounced lightly down the steps to the sea. "Dilo, I'm coming," she called out as she put on her mask and snorkel. As soon as she was in the sea Debra dived down to the seabed and picked up two stones. She banged them together. She knew Dilo would recognise her secret signal. When Dilo didn't appear she continued swimming clapping the stones as she went. No Dilo. Eventually she swam back to the rocks.

Pat saw Debra's disappointment as soon as

she stepped back into the house. "He's probably far out in the bay catching his breakfast. Sit down and have yours. You can try again later," he said optimistically.

And that's just what Debra did. Several times she swam out from the rocks. But no Dilo. Debra persuaded Pat to row her to The Silent Pool, the secret cave where she knew Dilo rested, but the dolphin wasn't there. She got Mike, her diver friend, to search far and wide in his inflatable. Reluctantly she had to accept that Dilo had gone away.

The next day Uncle Pat and Postie racked their brains to fathom out why Dilo should have disappeared. They considered the possibility that he had swum off to find a mate. They asked the fishermen coming back into the harbour if they had seen Dilo on their visits to the fishing grounds. But none of them had. How and why the friendly dolphin had disappeared remained a complete mystery.

Time went by. At first the fishermen left out their signs, TRIPS TO SEE THE DOLPHIN, in the hope Dilo would return. After several days they took them down.

Robin and his Uncle Pat continued to record the details of the wildlife and the boating activity in the harbour on the International Wildlife Watch computer. Then, one day when she was in the observation room with her brother, Debra commented, "Robin, if that computer of yours is so clever, why can't it tell us what happened to Dilo?"

It was meant as a joke, Debra wasn't keen on computers. Even so, Debra's remark inspired Robin to call up every observation he had made on Dilo. He tried to connect Dilo's disappearance with the phases of the moon, with the presence of seals, with the weather, but nothing gave him a clue.

Robin tried linking Dilo to 'Boating Activity', but nothing seemed to tie up. Dilo obviously liked boats. The more boating activity there was, the more Dilo jumped and moved around the bay.

Debra watched the screen intently, "Can't

you come up with anything?" she asked.

"No, not a thing," Robin said with a hopeless shrug of his shoulders.

"After your dream I even looked up witches on the world wide web, but I couldn't find out any thing about the Witch of Black Rock" Then he thought for a moment. "There is one small thing," he added. "Do you remember *Sea Wolf?* There was something very suspicious about that boat. Well, on the day before Dilo vanished it was in the bay. What's more, it had an unusual net on board."

"*Sea Wolf* is not a fishing boat, so why did it have a net on board?" asked Pat, who had joined them.

"You don't think those men on *Sea Wolf* have caught Dilo?" asked Debra with a horrified look on her face.

"What would they have done with him if they had?" added Pat. "People don't eat dolphins. Well not in this part of the world anyway."

"Some people still watch dolphin shows," said Postie who had arrived and joined in the conversation.

"You don't think they've caught Dilo and taken him to an aquarium?" suggested Pat.

They were all surprised that none of them had seriously considered this possibility before.

"Performing dolphins fetch a high price," added Postie. He thought about it for a moment before he continued. "I'll have to do some research. I've got a friend in London who may be able to help. When I get home I'll look up his number and give him a call."

Robin was quiet. Debra recognised the signs.

"Robin, you look as if you are going to have one of your brain waves," she said.

"I've already had it Sis," he replied, looking very excited. "There are things called Electronic Bulletin Boards. If we put out an appeal for information about Dilo on the International Wildlife Watch website someone is sure to pick it up." He looked at Postie for confirmation. "That's right isn't it?"

"So I believe. There's no harm in giving it

a try anyway."

"If computers can help us find Dilo I will never say anything against them ever again," added Debra, pleased to have some new hope of finding her beloved dolphin friend.

11

Daisy

Daisy the dolphin lived on her own in the aquarium in Crookhaven. When she first arrived there were arguments about where Daisy came from, and who owned her. To make sure that there were no disputes in the future, the curator had a daisy shape branded on her dorsal fin.

During the day Daisy did her shows in the display area. After each performance she would swim into a tiny holding pool. A metal grill would be pulled across the entrance. She would stay there until her next show.

Daisy spent most of her time swimming in circles. She remembered the time when she could swim in a straight line in the open sea, but that was long ago. Daisy had been captured when she was young. Now the humans who controlled her life were her family and friends. Tina, one of the trainers, was the human she liked most of all.

Daisy would do anything to please Tina.

There was a time when Daisy had a dolphin friend. He was called Boomps. Boomps came from another aquarium. He had been to lots of aquariums.

Daisy always did what her trainer signalled. But sometimes Boomps would do something different for no reason at all. Often he would swim around the pool at high speed, jump high in the air and fall backwards into the water with an enormous splash. Then, like two conspirators, Boomps and Daisy would stay underwater pretending they couldn't see the signals of the trainer who was trying to get them to do their routine. Daisy enjoyed doing shows with Boomps. Then he became ill and died quite suddenly.

Daisy was very sad. After Boomps had gone she wanted to be with Tina, her favourite trainer, more than ever. The nights were an awful time for Daisy. She would feel very lonely. She remembered the time when there were stars in the sky. Now all she could see overhead was the dim roof over her pool.

Each morning Daisy would wait to feel the first vibrations through the water. It was the sound she had been waiting for all through the lonely night. It was the sign that humans were coming. First she would hear distant doors opening. After that came the clatter of the fish bucket as the trainers prepared for the show.

When music poured out of loud speakers Daisy knew the show was about to begin. That excited her. She would swim faster and faster around her tiny enclosure. With nothing else to occupy her mind, the show was the one thing she lived for.

Daisy loved people, especially her trainers. She jumped and swam to please them. They fed her. But above all else, after her night in solitude, it was contact with humans she craved for most of all.

Every day throughout the summer season was the same. Daisy waited for what she knew would happen next. The music would stop. Then an announcement would blare out of the loud speakers.

"Ladies and gentlemen, boys and girls," it boomed. "The moment you have been waiting for is here. Give a big Crookhaven welcome to the star of the show - Daisy the dolphin!"

At that moment the iron grill that had kept her confined to her overnight quarters would be pulled aside and Daisy would swim into the main pool. She would circle the pool twice and then rear out of the water by the platform and open her mouth to receive her first fish of the day.

The audience always cheered when she did this. The trainer on the platform held a microphone in one hand. In her mouth she had a whistle, like a dog whistle, which the audience could only just hear but was very loud to the dolphin.

The trainer would then point with her free hand. Daisy would wait for a moment, poised for her next move. Then, when the whistle blew, she would swim round the pool and jump over a pole which the trainer held out over the water. Daisy would then instantly return to the platform for a

reward of fish.

Daisy's routine included jumping through hoops and taking a fish from her trainer's outstretched hand. After that Daisy would surface beside the platform with her mouth wide open.

"Like all good children Daisy has to have her teeth cleaned after a meal," the trainer would comment as she produced a huge toothbrush and pretended to clean Daisy's teeth.

Daisy's next trick was to squirt water out of her mouth at the children along the edge of the pool - who always shrieked with surprise. Everyone laughed.

"Oh you naughty dolphin," shouted the trainer. "Tell the boys and girls you are sorry."

The trainer would then give another signal and Daisy would rear her head out of the water and squeak so that everyone could hear her. As soon as she had done that, Daisy would rush back to the platform for another fish.

"Now I want a boy or girl from the audience to volunteer to go for a ride with Daisy."

There was never any shortage of

volunteers. The trainer would then throw a small inflated boat into the pool. A child would be put into the boat. Daisy would then take the rope in her mouth and tow the boat around the pool.

At the end of the show the trainer would turn the fish bucket upside down to show the audience, and Daisy, that it was empty. When the crowd had filed out, Daisy would go back to her pen and the gate would be closed. There would be no more rewards until the next performance.

Daisy went through the same routine every day, four times a day, except on the day Dilo arrived. That was different.

12

What kind of place is this?

When Dilo was taken to the aquarium he was lowered into a tiny pool separated from the main pool by a metal grill. He was pleased to be back in the water again where he could breathe more easily. Dilo swam in a circle around the small enclosure. Despite his ordeal Dilo was remarkably fit.

As he recovered his strength and his temperature became steady, Dilo's impulse was to explore his surroundings. That was what his mother had taught him to do whenever he went somewhere new. In the open sea the first thing he always did was to scan with his long distance sonar. This told him the size and position of the rocks in the area. Then, using his eyes and another type of sonar, he would go exploring. He would poke his nose, or beak, into caves - after making sure there were no large lobsters lurking inside of course. Dilo would investigate the gulleys and the sandy seabed between the rocks. In this way he would soon build-up a mental map of the region and store it in his remarkable memory. Dilo depended upon this for his survival in the sea.

But life was not just about survival for Dilo - he could do that easily. It was about being curious, about being alive, about having fun. The very act of experiencing everything around him made Dilo feel good. He felt pleasure when he saw seaweeds clinging to rocks - especially when the water was rough and they were flung around in the sea's fury. He would rush through the wild foam, feeling the sea's energy.

When the sea was calm he would glide serenely through the placid water. The sight of ribbons of sunlight dancing on the rocks filled him with peace. For Dilo, the joy of just being alive in a place as wondrous as the sea, made him very happy.

When Dilo turned on his magic sound in

the aquarium, it bounced off the concrete walls and came back as a booming echo. There were no nooks or crannies to explore. So he turned off his sound. His eyes were stinging with the chlorine in the water. When he opened them there were no shapes or movements to see. Wherever he looked he saw plain white walls. There was no tide.

" What kind of place have these humans brought me to?" the dolphin asked himself. He swam to the iron grill that stopped him going into the big pool. He could not see through the cloudy water to the other side but he felt there was another presence. He beamed his sonar across the flat concrete bottom. It showed him that on the far side was another iron grill. Something was moving behind the grill. It was another dolphin in a tiny holding pool, just like his.

13

Come on Daisy

Daisy was aware that something different was happening on the morning Dilo was stranded on the beach. The doors of the aquarium were opened early. There was lots of human activity. She heard Dilo being lowered into the other holding pool. When Daisy heard Dilo's sonar it stirred something inside her. Dilo's sound immediately brought back memories of her former friend, Boomps, and the dolphins she swam with in the sea when she was young.

Daisy swam to the grill and sent her own sonar across the pool towards Dilo. The two dolphins excitedly exchanged signals. Dilo and Daisy pressed their beaks against the iron bars. They wanted to get closer, to swim together and to see one another. But they were kept apart, each in their own tiny pool.

Eventually Daisy heard the sound she was

waiting for. Music. Daisy kept swimming excitedly round her pool and then pressing her beak against the metal grill. At last the gate was drawn back.

Daisy rushed out and swam across the show pool to the other enclosure. Dilo had his beak pressed hard against the grill. He wriggled his body with delight when Daisy swam into view.

Tina, the trainer, blew her whistle. Daisy could hear it through the water but she ignored the call for the show to begin. Daisy was much more interested in making contact with Dilo. The whistle blew again and again. Daisy stayed underwater. She circled in front of Dilo who watched her through the bars.

"I'm afraid Daisy is distracted by the dolphin we rescued from the beach this morning," came the voice of Tina over the loudspeaker.

"Come on Daisy, show the boys and girls how you can jump."

Daisy ignored the request. She rose to the surface, snatched a breath and descended immediately.

"Come on Daisy," pleaded the trainer. "It's time for breakfast."

Tina threw a fish into the water. Daisy saw it drifting downwards but took no notice. Another fish followed.

"If you don't come and see me I shall be very upset," said the trainer blowing her whistle once again.

Daisy stayed underwater swimming back and forth past Dilo.

"Alright then, I shall leave you," said the voice over the loudspeaker.

Daisy did her shows because she wanted to please Tina and the visitors who came to the pool. Today she was torn between being close to Dilo and obeying the commands of the whistle and the hand signals. Daisy was very upset when her trainer walked off the platform. She wanted to please her favourite human friend so much.

Tina came back to the platform a short time later. Through the water Daisy saw Tina's hand signal. Then she heard the whistle.

"Come on Daisy, please show the boys and

girls how you can jump," came the voice over the loudspeaker.

Daisy could resist no longer. She swam round the pool and popped up in front of her trainer.

"Good girl," said Tina as she popped a fish into Daisy's open mouth.

As soon as she had swallowed the fish Daisy swam back to Dilo. When the whistle blew again Daisy did another trick and then swam quickly back and forth infront of Dilo. Daisy did do other parts of her show but spent most of the time underwater. At the end she towed the boat with a child in it to the middle of the pool and then let go of the rope to return to Dilo. Tina jumped into the pool and pulled the boat back to the platform.

When all the spectators had left the man who had arrived on the beach, just after Beth and Ann had found Dilo, rushed onto the platform. He was angry.

"That was an utter shambles," he shouted at Tina. " I thought you were supposed to be a trainer," he raged. " Don't give that animal any more food until it obeys your commands instantly," he said pointing at Daisy.

"Oh, and another thing," he added, pointing at Dilo. "You'd better start training that dolphin right away. I want it in the show as soon as possible."

14

Star

The process of training Dilo to become a dolphin clown began immediately. Dilo learned quickly. He had Daisy to show him. At first Dilo did not like eating dead fish, but coaxed by Tina he gradually accepted them.

Tina got into the water with Dilo the first time he was let into the main pool for a training session. Dilo liked Tina. In some ways she reminded him of Debra. Tina was surprised and pleased when Dilo let her touch him straight away. Tina was even more delighted when she got hold of Dilo's dorsal fin and he towed her through the water. Never before had a newly-captured dolphin allowed her to do that so soon.

Tina soon realised there was something extra special about Dilo. After they had been together for several days Tina was surprised to see a faint star on Dilo's dorsal fin. "Why didn't I notice that when you first came into the aquarium?" she asked herself.

Her boss, the man on the beach, came to the pool during some training sessions. At all other times he stayed in his office. He didn't want Beth and Ann to know he was the manager, or curator, of the aquarium.

"We'll have to give it a name," he said to Tina when she told him how quickly Dilo was learning to jump and do somersaults on her commands.

"Let's call him Star," she suggested, "because of the star on his dorsal fin."

"I can't see no star," said the man.

"That's funny," said Tina. "I couldn't at first, but now I can see it quite clearly."

"You'd better get your eyes tested. Star's a good name anyway," said the man. "Star can become the star of the show," he chuckled. He was pleased with his little joke.

Beth and Ann went to the aquarium every day to find out how Dilo was getting on. They became friendly with Tina. They would stay behind when all the other spectators had gone.

The two girls watched as Tina encouraged Dilo, or Star as he was now called, to perform more and more tricks. When nobody was around Tina let Beth and Ann use her whistle and do hand signals. They were delighted when Dilo responded. Tina told them not to tell anyone as it was strictly against the rules.

Although Beth and Ann enjoyed every minute they spent at the aquarium something troubled them.

"Tina," said Beth, "when we discovered Star we wanted to put him back into the sea. It's been lovely being so close to him in the pool, but don't you think Star really belongs in the sea?"

"Maybe you're right," replied Tina, "but he does seem to enjoy being in the pool with Daisy and he does bring pleasure to lots of people.

"I know," said Beth, "but it still doesn't feel right to me."

15

Postie's plan

Two days before the children were due to leave the lighthouse, everyone gathered in the kitchen. There was an air of great excitement. Boka the dog sensed it and was running around going nowhere. Only Sprat the cat didn't seem to be bothered - he was fast asleep in front of the stove. Everyone had some news. Postie started.

"My friend in London has turned up some interesting information on *Sea Wolf* . It is owned by a man who is suspected of drug dealing and gun running. That's one of the reasons why he's got such a fast boat. He's a clever crook. So far nobody has been able to prove anything, and he is very good at laundering money."

"What does laundering money mean?" asked Debra.

"It doesn't mean putting it in a washing machine," piped up Robin.

"I know that," said Debra annoyed at her brother's interruption.

"It means putting money from crime into respectable businesses," answered Postie.

"Then nobody asks questions about where the money came from?" said Debra.

"Quite right," replied Postie.

"Well this man has his money well spread around, but here's the important point. He part owns an aquarium at Crookhaven - and the aquarium has a dolphin show."

"How many dolphins are there at Crookhaven?" asked Debra.

"There were two, but one died. The one that's left is called Daisy. If she dies there will be no more shows." Postie paused. "And no more profits."

"So he could be interested in getting another dolphin," deduced Robin. " That ties in with the information we've got back from our Bulletin Board. Somebody has seen a newspaper report about a stranded dolphin. And guess where it was taken afterwards - to Crookhaven

Aquarium."

" What else did you find out Robin?" asked Debra eagerly.

"They've given it a name. Star." replied Robin. "What's more, Star was found stranded on the beach at Crookhaven one day after Dilo disappeared from Lighthouse Bay."

"Well if Dilo was caught by *Sea Wolf* and taken to Crookhaven, proving it could be difficult," said Pat.

"Crookhaven is a long way away. Surely Dilo wouldn't have swum that far and then stranded himself on the beach," argued Robin.

Then Debra remembered the dream she had the night Dilo disappeared. She could still see it clearly in her mind. Debra told everyone about her nightmare and how the Witch of Black Rock had cast a spell over Dilo and turned him into a crow.

"When I woke up and looked out of the window I thought I saw a boat out by Black Rock. But I can't be sure if it was *Sea Wolf*. I didn't think it was important at the time."

"First we've got to find out if Star is Dilo,"

said Postie.

"And if Star is Dilo, then we'll have to work out a plan of action to put him back in to the sea. That's where he belongs," added Debra emphatically.

"I've got a proposal," said Postie. "I'm on holiday next week. Why don't I go to Crookhaven and see the situation for myself?"

"Can I come with you?" asked Debra.

"Me too?" asked Robin.

"I thought you two were supposed to be at school next week?" Postie remembered.

"We are," said Debra, " but finding out what has happened to Dilo is much more important than lessons."

"This is a lesson in life," added Robin. "I'm sure Mum would agree."

Robin was good at persuading his mother if he wanted something really badly.

"What do you think Pat?" asked Postie.

"I think it's a good plan if Mary agrees. A few days off school won't do these two any harm."

"I'm sure she will, I'm sure she will," said

Debra excitedly.

"You will have to make up for it by working extra hard afterwards," added Pat, looking directly at the twins and wagging a finger at them.

"Oh we will, we will," said Debra enthusiastically, having already decided that if Robin and his uncle asked, her mother could not possibly say 'No'.

Postie, who managed a big factory before he decided to become a postman, was a good organiser. Four days later he and the twins were in the audience at the dolphin circus in Crookhaven.

16

A slippery customer

Debra recognised Dilo the instant he swam into the big pool. Postie had difficulty stopping Debra from running onto the platform during the show. When it was over they asked to see the person in charge. They were shown into the office of the man on the beach. He was very polite. Postie was polite also.

He started by saying, "We have come to enquire when and how you propose to return Star to the sea."

"Who said we should return Star to the sea?"

"Well that's where he belongs and it's illegal to take a dolphin out of the sea without a special permit. Do you have a permit?"

"We didn't take the dolphin out of the sea. It was stranded on the beach. It's a sick dolphin and we are looking after it. We saved its life." he said.

Debra couldn't keep quiet. "It doesn't look sick to me," she said curtly.

"I can assure you it is," the man said, still smiling. Then he became serious. "Our vet has taken blood samples and says the dolphin is under stress."

"So would you be if you were kept in a prison," Debra retorted.

The man had difficulty staying calm. But he managed to.

"What a silly little girl you are. Can't you see that Star is better off here? He gets plenty of food. There are no sharks to bother him. I bet if you were a dolphin you would rather be in this cosy pool than out in open sea."

"Oh no I wouldn't!" came the sharp reply.

Postie could see that Debra was getting cross. He thought it best if everyone stayed calm.

"We have reason to believe the dolphin you call Star is in fact a friendly wild dolphin named Dilo," he said firmly.

"I've never heard such rubbish," said the

man beginning to lose his politeness. "Even if Star is Dilo, you could never prove it."

He immediately realised this was not a wise thing to have said and stood up.

"I'm sorry I'm a very busy man. I must ask you to leave. I can assure you that the dolphin we rescued is enjoying its stay here," he said seriously. "Thank you for calling - and for expressing your concern. We all want what's best for the dolphin." He opened the door. " I hope you enjoy the rest of your holiday," he said smiling once again as he ushered Postie and the twins out of the door.

When they were outside Debra let her anger show.

"What a creep," she said indignantly.

"I think he's more interested in the welfare of his wallet than he is of the dolphin," said Postie.

"What a slippery customer he is," added Robin. "I didn't believe a word he said. I wouldn't trust him to look after our cat. We've got to work out a plan to rescue Dilo."

The moment he shut the door the man's

expression changed. He looked annoyed. He went to the telephone and dialled *Sea Wolf.*

"I've just had a man here with a couple of brats in tow," he said urgently. "They've been asking awkward questions about the dolphin you delivered. They want to know when it's going to be put back in the sea."

"That's a very valuable animal, I didn't go to all that trouble just to let it go again. It's up to you to make sure that the dolphin is *not* put back into the sea. Feed it some bad fish and then get the vet to examine it. Give it an injury if you have to. That dolphin stays in the aquarium. If it doesn't, you can look for a new job. What do you think we pay you for?" he shouted angrily before slamming the phone back into its holder.

17

Detective work

As soon as they left the aquarium Postie phoned Pat and told him what had happened.

"Well, I've got news for you," replied Pat "*Sea Wolf* is back in the bay. The customs men have been on board. They didn't find any drugs or guns. But guess what they found? Diving gear. An underwater scooter. A net. And a canvas sling, of the type used for transporting dolphins"

"There is nothing illegal in that," replied Postie.

"I know," said Pat. "But it does look very suspicious."

"What are you going to do now?" asked Pat.

" I'm not sure," replied Postie. " We'll have to work out a plan."

"Well, be careful. The people you are dealing with are dangerous," added Pat before putting down the phone.

"If only Dilo could talk," said Debra when they were all sitting down for their evening meal, " he could tell us what really happened."

"Do you think if we could prove Dilo was stolen, he would have to be put back into the sea?" asked Robin

"Well the law says you have to have a special licence to take a dolphin out of the sea and put it in an aquarium. So if we could prove what they did was illegal, then there is a good chance Dilo would be put back."

"So we need to do some detective work," said Robin.

"Where do we start?" asked Debra.

"At the newspaper office," replied Postie.

By the end of the day Postie and the twins had tracked down Beth and Ann. The trio called in at their house. Ann told them what had happened.

"In the paper it said we telephoned Crookhaven aquarium. They got it wrong. We never did that. A friendly man we met on the beach did. Then a team from the aquarium came. We said we wanted to put Star back in the sea."

Ann had a suggestion. "The trainer at the aquarium is very friendly. Her name is Tina, she might help."

"We haven't got long to sort this mess out," said Postie. "It's Thursday now and I told your mother you would be back on Sunday."

"We could do with some inside information on the aquarium," said Robin who liked playing detective.

"Suppose instead of helping us, Tina tells that awful man?" wondered Debra.

"I think we'll have to take that risk," said Postie. " Perhaps you should try and make friends with Tina. You're good at that Debbie."

They agreed it would look less suspicious if only one of them went to the aquarium. So the next day Debra went to see the performance. The sight of Dilo jumping filled her with joy. But at the same time she was very sad to see him locked in a pool. To Debra it seemed that Dilo was in a prison.

When the performance was over, Debra slipped quietly behind the scenes where she found

Tina. The trainer was weighing out fish for the next show. Tina was friendly.

" Each dolphin gets a strict ration," she said.

Debra asked about the bottles of pills beside the sink in which frozen fish were being thawed.

"Dead fish don't have all the vitamins the dolphins need," explained Tina. " So I put the pills inside the fish. Each dolphin has a strict ration of pills as well as fish. I keep all the records in this book," she continued, showing Debra the book.

"That's very unnatural isn't it?" said Debra cautiously.

"Yes it is," said Tina, "but it is essential if the dolphins are to stay healthy."

Debra liked Tina and decided to risk telling her about Dilo and why she had come to the aquarium. Tina listened intently. She paused for a time, thinking.

"The day before Star was found on the beach I was told to get out the equipment we use for moving a dolphin. It was at the back of the store room. We hadn't used it for ages. At the time I didn't think any more about it. But it all makes sense now if what you say is true."

"Then will you help us put Dilo back in the sea?" Debra asked finally.

"Yes, I will if I can," replied Tina. "You had better go now before anyone sees you here."

"I will be back tomorrow with Beth and Ann," said Debra as she left.

When Debra had gone, Tina went to the holding pool where Dilo was swimming slowly around in a circle. When she saw him she felt very sorry for the dolphin. Debra had told her how Dilo loved to poke his nose into the caves and how he swam under seaweeds and sometimes chased fishes over the sand. Now all he had were flat walls, a concrete floor and dead fish to eat.

Tina squatted down beside the pool. Dilo swam over to her and raised his head out of the water.

"Oh Star," said Tina, "What have we done to you? You're so beautiful."

Tina gently stroked Dilo's throat. She felt

his smooth, silky skin slipping under her fingers.

"I love you and I shall miss you. I know your home is really in the sea. How can we put you back? I don't know, but I'm sure we can find a way."

18

Fearsome Fivesome

"Now the Terrible Twins have become a Fearsome Foursome," said Postie with a smile when Debra, Robin, Beth and Ann gathered on the beach for a council of war the next day.

"We're the Fearsome Fivesome if we count you as well," said Robin looking at Postie.

"And we're ready for action," said Debra.

A short time later they were all at the aquarium. They didn't go to the pool. Instead they went to the office area. One of the doors had a sign: CURATOR. Postie knocked.

"Come in."

Postie opened the door. Beth and Ann, recognised the person standing in the room instantly. It was the friendly man on the beach. He recognised them too. He looked very surprised, but he quickly recovered his composure.

"Well this is a surprise. How nice to see

you again," he said looking at Beth and Ann, smiling falsely.

"We've come to set Dilo free," said Debra, unable to control her anger.

The man ignored her. He continued to look at Beth and Ann.

"Unfortunately you've caught me at a bad time. I'm very busy right now, goodbye." he said starting to close the door.

"Busy making money out of our beautiful friendly dolphin," said Debra hotly.

Postie took hold of the door handle.

"I think you had better hear what we have to say," said Postie stopping the curator from closing the door.

The man backed away and the Fearsome Fivesome moved in and closed around him. Ann and Beth told him he had lied to the newspaper. They all pleaded for Dilo to be returned to the sea. The man refused their request outright.

Finally Postie said firmly, "Diving equipment and nets that could have been used for catching a dolphin have been found on a boat called *Sea Wolf.* And *Sea Wolf* was seen in Lighthouse Bay just before Dilo disappeared.

"What you say may be true," said the man sharply, "but it doesn't prove anything." He paused "The dolphin was injured and stranded on the beach. Until you can prove otherwise, Star stays. Now you can all go," he said curtly, pushing the Fearesome Fivesome out of the door and slamming it behind them.

"What on earth are we going to do?" said Debra as they walked down the corridor. "We haven't got much time left."

"We could try and get Dilo out tonight. Perhaps Tina would help us, she knows where all the equipment is," suggested Robin excitedly.

"They will be on guard now they know our intention," said Postie. " There is bound to be an alarm system. If the police were called in they would have to stop us from trespassing - that's their job."

"I know it is," said Debra angrily, "but that awful man stole Dilo from the sea."

"I'm afraid the police wouldn't see it that

way," said Postie.

"We can't give up now. We've got to think of something," said Debra determinedly.

The Fearsome Fivesome all had tea and cakes together. They remained glum. Nobody could think how to solve the problem.

19

A ray of hope

Postie called Pat at the lighthouse and told his friend the situation.

"I'm glad you've called," said Pat. " I've got some good news. I had a visitor a short time ago. It was Mike, our diving friend. He met a member of the crew of *Sea Wolf* in the pub. He told Mike how he got into the water after dark and managed to get Dilo to swim into a net."

"Why did he tell Mike all this?" asked Postie.

"He'd had a lot to drink."

"Do you think he would tell the police what happened?"

"I'm not sure. Mike said that the skipper of *Sea Wolf* is a very nasty piece of work. I wouldn't like to be in the diver's shoes if he did."

"Well, if he won't tell the police we're almost back to where we started."

"Not quite," replied Postie. "I've contacted International Wildlife Watch. They have said they will take legal advice and run a FREE DILO campaign."

"That could take ages, and we are only here for another couple of days," responded Postie.

"I know," said Pat. "but there is a ray of hope. I asked Mike to ask the diver to come to Crookhaven and see Dilo in the pool. I thought if Debra talked to him she could persuade him to join the FREE DILO campaign."

"Do you really think he will come?" asked Postie.

"I don't know. I just don't know," replied Pat.

20

Unexpected help

On their last day in Crookhaven, the Fearsome Fivesome decided to go back to the aquarium. Postie reluctantly bought tickets for the first performance.

When Dilo swam into the main pool he recognised Debra immediately. He kept breaking off from his routine to swim or jump close to her. Then, just after the show had started, Dilo saw a man sit down quietly beside Debra. It was the diver from *Sea Wolf.*

When the show was over Debra started to cry. "Oh Postie," she wailed between sniffles, "how can we go home and leave Dilo in this awful prison?"

Postie put his arm around her. Before he could reply the man sitting next to Debra, who had also stayed behind, spoke.

"Hello," he said "I'm Ted Manson. I'm the

diver who helped to catch Dilo and put him in 'prison' as you call it."

"Well, now you've seen him, what are you going to do about it?" asked Debra, brushing the tears from her cheeks.

" I've seen the kind of life Dilo leads here and I've decided to help you get him out."

"How?"

"I'm going to threaten to tell the authorities what really happened."

"Come on then," said Postie before the man changed his mind. "Let's go and see the curator again."

They stood up. But before they could move they were approached by two men. One of them was the curator.

" I heard you were back," he said. "This is my legal advisor."

"I'm glad you've brought him," said Postie, " because I think you are going to need his advice. This is Mr Manson," Postie continued, introducing the diver. "He is the man who caught Dilo in a net. Furthermore he is prepared to testify he did so. In a court of law if necessary."

The diver then explained to everyone how Dilo had been captured during the night in Lighthouse Bay and then taken to Crookhaven. When he had finished the two men went to one side and had a serious whispered discussion. Eventually they returned.

"My client says that there seems to have been a misunderstanding. He says he always intended to return the dolphin to the sea once it had recovered from it's unfortunate ordeal on the beach," said the lawyer with gravity.

"And *when* does your client intend to return the dolphin to the sea?" asked Debra abruptly.

"That depends," said the lawyer cautiously.

"Depends upon what?" responded Debra instantly.

"It depends upon whether or not Mr Manson wishes to make a statement about what allegedly happened before the dolphin was found on the beach."

"Carry on," said Debra looking him

straight in the face.

"If Mr Manson decides to go to the authorities then a lengthy legal situation could ensue, during which time the dolphin would, of course, remain in the aquarium."

"And what if he doesn't?" said Debra curtly.

"Should Mr Manson agree not to make any public accusations against my client, whose intention, I emphasise, has always been to return the dolphin to it's natural environment, then my client would be prepared to give the matter top priority.."

"What you are saying," said Postie, " is that if we keep quiet about what happened, Dilo would be put back into the sea immediately."

"Litigation, as you know, is a long and costly exercise. I do therefore strongly recommend this course of action." He paused. Then continued. " I am sure the media will find the release of the dolphin of interest. You and your friends would appear in the newspapers and on television. And the aquarium would benefit from the propagation of it's ideals as sanctuary for sick sea mammals, as well as a place for education and entertainment."

"What you are saying is that releasing the dolphin would be good publicity for your aquarium?" responded Postie.

"And would not your good selves find the experience agreeable?" questioned the lawyer with a false smile.

"Please tell your client that our *good selves* do not want to publicise his wretched aquarium. We do want Dilo put back in the sea immediately," responded Debra hotly.

"Do I take it that this young lady's view is shared by you all?" enquired the lawyer.

Everyone nodded. "Then I am sure my client will see to the matter immediately."

"Tell your client that we don't trust him," sparked Debra. "And that we want to be there when it happens."

The two men went into a huddle again.

"My client feels it may take some time to capture the dolphin. The usual procedure is to lower the water in the pool and that takes a full day."

"Tell your client that will not be necessary," retorted Debra. "I will persuade Dilo to go into the sling."

"You, madam?" said the lawyer raising his eyebrows.

"Yes me. In case you didn't know, Dilo and I are good friends. He will do what I wish if I ask him nicely."

"Ask him, madam?" said the lawyer disbelievingly - once again raising his eyebrows.

"Yes, ask him," said Debra with a pained expression on her face. It seemed obvious to her that Dilo would co-operate if it would lead to his freedom.

21

Going home

Dilo was surprised when Debra slid quietly into his holding pool. At first he was excited and swam round her quickly. Debra matched him by swimming like a dolphin with her legs together. Gradually she slowed down. So did Dilo. Then Ted Manson, the diver, and Tina, the trainer got into the pool. Dilo swam to them and then went back to Debra. The stretcher with two holes was lowered gently into the water. Dilo inspected it and swam away. Tina and Ted remained quiet and calm. They did not want to alarm Dilo. Debra stroked Dilo very gently and spoke to him in a quiet voice.

"Come on Dilo, do this for me. I've told them you would. Just swim over the stretcher. There is no hurry. Then we will lift you out of this awful pool and put you back in the sea, where you belong."

Those around the pool watched in silence. Could Debra entice a dolphin to do something he would not normally do? Did Dilo trust Debra that much?

Dilo behaved almost as if he were asleep. He hung on the surface of the pool with Debra stroking him.

"Come on Dilo, I know we can do it," she said in a whisper.

Tina and the diver moved slowly towards her. Gently they started to slide the stretcher beneath Dilo. The dolphin swam away. Debra's plan wasn't working.

Debra continued to talk to Dilo, "Please Dilo, stay still, please, do it for me." Tina and Ted edged forwards. "Please stay still Dilo, please," pleaded Debra.

Dilo obeyed. Very slowly the sling was raised under Dilo. Debra gently guided Dilo's pectoral fins through the holes especially made for the purpose.

Dilo was caught.

The three moved to the edge of the pool.

DOLPHINARIUM

Debra continued to talk to Dilo, pacifying him with her words. Two more assistants came into the water.

With one person on each corner of the stretcher Dilo was heaved out of the pool. Soon he was being carried to a waiting van. After a short ride on a foam mattress Dilo was lifted out. Four strong people carried him down the beach.

Debra, still wearing her wetsuit, walked by his side, "You're going home. You're going back to the sea," she said excitedly.

As he was lowered into the sea Dilo felt cool sea water bathe his body. His weight was gone. It was easy to breathe. Dilo didn't struggle as he was eased into deeper water. Then the magic moment came. The stretcher was slipped from under him and the four men waded ashore.

Dilo remained floating, bobbing gently on the surface. Next to him was Debra. She too floated gently on the surface, comfortable in her wetsuit. Occasionally she blew out through her snorkel tube. Dilo closed his eyes. His body was soaking in the sounds of the sea - the crackle of the shrimps, the coarse grating sound of the waves rolling up the beach and the distant throb of an engine. He could sense Debra floating beside him. She wasn't touching him but he knew exactly where she was. He also knew she would not stay long. She was a visitor to the sea from the land.

Then he remembered his mother, telling him he was born to roam. 'The Call of the Deep' she called it. At that moment of freedom he felt it stronger than ever. He loved having Debra beside him but he knew it was time to leave the shore and head out into the wide, wide ocean. The thought of it filled him with energy and joy. He opened his eyes and started to swim around Debra. Faster and faster he went until he was travelling at full speed. He dived to the bottom and rubbed his belly on the coarse sand. Then he headed for the surface and leapt as high as he could. He felt the air on his body before he crashed back into the sea in a tumult of bubbles.

Throughout his stay in the pool Dilo had swum in circles. Now he could swim in a straight line. And that's what he did. He left Debra and swam at full speed towards the horizon. Occasionally Dilo jumped just for the sheer joy of once again being free in the sea.

22

The Daisy appeal

When Debra swam back to the beach she was surprised to find herself facing a television camera crew and a reporter. She was furious. The curator of the aquarium had said he wouldn't make a publicity stunt out of Dilo's return to the sea. He had broken his word. The camera crew had remained hidden and filmed the whole thing. Now they wanted to interview Debra.

"Hello," said a lady interviewer, holding a microphone in front of Debra. "You've obviously got a special friendship with dolphins. Would you like to tell us about Star?"

Debra didn't have time to consider her reply carefully. "Yes," she said, "I've known him for a long time and I don't call him Star, I call him Dilo."

"Oh do you," said the reporter, "Where did you first meet Star, I mean Dilo?"

"I met Dilo a long way from here, in Lighthouse Bay."

Once she got going, Debra forgot about the fact that she was being filmed. She talked excitedly of how magical it was to swim with Dilo in the open sea and how many adventures they had had together.

"These are wonderful stories. You are a very lucky girl to have a wild dolphin as a friend," said the interviewer. "You are obviously pleased to see Dilo back in the sea but what do you think about Daisy?"

"I don't think any dolphin should be kept in a concrete pool," said Debra vehemently. " I think it is cruel. Daisy should be set free."

"Thank you very much Debra," said the reporter, closing the interview.

"That was a good controversial note to end on," she commented to the crew as they packed away their equipment. "Let's go back to the studio and edit it right away."

That evening the four children gathered, with Postie and Ted, to watch Dilo's return to the sea. Debra wasn't at all sure she liked seeing herself on television.

At the end of the interview the reporter spoke directly to the camera. "As you can see, Debra feels strongly about keeping dolphins in captivity. What do you think? Should Daisy be kept penned up in a tiny pool, or should she be set free? Let us hear your views."

"Well, that will set the cat amongst the pigeons," said Postie. "I reckon that most people believe dolphins should be free. I bet they write in and say so. I don't think the aquarium owners will be very happy about that."

Postie was right, there was an enormous public response. A film crew was sent to interview Pat at the lighthouse. A SET DAISY FREE campaign was launched by International Wildlife Watch. Thousands of people, especially children, signed petitions. Supporters of the campaign were filmed parading outside the aquarium. Beth and Amy joined in. They held up placards which said: DOLPHINS BELONG IN THE SEA.

23

Moving with the times

The protest was so successful the aquarium started to lose money. After many consultations and strong arguments with the angry owner, the curator called a press conference. He told Tina to be present. Putting on his pleasant public face, he announced, "The aquarium is moving with the times. We are turning the Dolphin Pool into a Human Pool," He paused. Nobody spoke.

"Crookhaven will have a state-of-the-art swimming pool with a flume and a wave machine."

"What will happen to Daisy?" asked a reporter.

"We shall put her back in the sea."

"Will she survive after spending so much time in captivity?"

"I will hand you over to Tina, her trainer, to answer that question."

"I have been in touch with International Wildlife Watch and we are making plans to take Daisy to an enclosure in a quiet bay where she will learn to catch fish again. When the time is right, we shall set her free," responded Tina.

"Won't that cost a lot of money?"

"Yes."

"Who will pay?"

"When International Wildlife Watch set up their FREE DAISY campaign, it received a very generous donation that will cover most of the costs," replied Tina.

"Who will look after Daisy whilst she is being rehabilitated?"

"I will," said Tina, " And I will be helped by Debra - the friend of the dolphin we called Star"

"Where exactly will you take Daisy?"

"To Lighthouse Bay."

And that is what happened...... except that the release of Daisy did not go exactly according to plan.

24

Daisy disappears

Daisy was transported in a van from the aquarium to Lighthouse Bay. Tina stayed beside Daisy throughout the entire journey, keeping the dolphin sprayed with water and talking to her.

"We are taking you home. We are taking you back to the sea," she said in a gentle, reassuring voice.

Robin and Debra were given time off school and were on the jetty when the van arrived.

The fishermen had made a net with a big mesh that fish could swim through. It had floats along the top and was weighted along the bottom. Earlier in the day they had strung it across the entrance to The Silent Pool.

Mike had explained to them, "Strange as it may seem, dolphins don't jump over nets. The net will keep Daisy safely inside The Silent Pool until she has learnt to catch live fish."

A fishing boat carried Daisy from the jetty to The Silent Pool. Debra and Tina changed into their wetsuits and were in the water when Daisy was gently lowered into the sea.

Daisy was relieved to be back in the water after her journey in the van. At first she stayed quietly on the surface with her two human friends by her side. The dolphin glided slowly around The Silent Pool sending out her sonar. It brought back memories of the time before she was captured.

Tina and Debra snorkelled down to Daisy as she explored her new territory. Mike stayed inside The Silent Pool, in his inflatable, ready to give a hand if any was needed. But it wasn't.

"Daisy loves her new home," Debra shouted to Mike. "She's swimming just like Dilo used to. I'm sure it won't be long before we can let her out."

Hours passed without Debra realising it. When dusk came Mike called out, "Come on girls. It's time to go. Don't worry, I'll bring you back tomorrow morning."

True to his word, early next morning Mike

arrived at the steps at the base of the Lighthouse with a bucket of freshly caught fish. Debra and Tina, dressed in their wetsuits, were ready and waiting. They talked excitedly as they examined the fish.

"Daisy must be hungry. I'm sure she'll love these," said Tina.

Mike switched off the engine and paddled into The Silent Pool which was surrounded by towering cliffs. It was quiet. The gulls stopped squawking. Everything was still. The inflatable floated like a leaf on a pond. Nobody spoke. They were all waiting to hear the "phft" that dolphins make when they come up to breathe. But no sound broke the silence. Something was wrong.

"Where's Daisy? she should have come to us," said Tina, expressing the concern that they all felt.

Mike looked around. There was no sign of the dolphin anywhere.

"You two had better get into the water and see if you can find her."

"I'll bang some stones together. That should

attract her," said Debra hopefully.

Tina and Debra swam from one end of The Silent Pool to the other and back again. There was no sign of the dolphin. Daisy had vanished. They were horrified. Mike, who was wearing a drysuit. pulled on his aqualung.

" You two come back on board." he said as he strapped on his weightbelt. "I'll dive down and inspect the net,"

Tina and Debra watched as Mike's bubbles burst up to the surface along the length of the net. Eventually he returned and hung on to one of the handles on the side of his inflatable.

"There's one place where the net is not touching the bottom. Daisy must have got out through there," he said, with a serious expression on his face as he unclipped his diving equipment.

Tina leaned over the side and heaved Mike's aqualung into the boat. Mike hauled himself aboard.

"It looks like we've lost Daisy," said Tina despondently.

"We'll go back to the lighthouse and I'll put

out a radio message to the fishermen and ask them to keep an eye out for her," said Mike.

Pat, Robin and Postie were all surprised when they saw the inflatable speeding back to the lighthouse so soon. Everyone was gloomy when Debra told them that Daisy had vanished.

"Perhaps Daisy has been captured by the Witch and is being kept prisoner inside Black Rock," suggested Robin.

Memories of the nightmare she had before Dilo was captured came flooding back to Debra.

"Oh please don't say that," pleaded Debra trying not to cry.

"The kettle's boiling. I'll get you some breakfast," said Pat.

"I'm too upset to eat. I've got the binoculars. I'm going outside," said Debra still trying to hold back her tears.

Outside Debra scanned the sea, still with a vision of the Witch of Black Rock sharp in her mind. A few minutes later she was back in the kitchen jumping up and down with excitement.

"I've seen her! I've seen her!" she shouted.

" Come on everyone. See for yourselves."

They all rushed outside and stood along the wall from which they had so often watched Dilo. And sure enough. There was Daisy. Near Black Rock. There was a flash of silver in the air. Then a splash.

"Did you see that? Did you see that?" squealed Debra jumping up and down, hysterical with delight. "Daisy has not been put under a spell by the Witch of Black Rock. She has caught a fish and is throwing it in the air, just like Dilo used to. She is showing us that she can catch fish. Daisy is telling us that she is pleased to be back in the wide open sea where she belongs."

THE END

Dear Reader

I started this book in a railway carriage on a trans Pennine journey from Ferriby to Manchester. At the airport I met my dear friend Rico to discuss the illustrations for *Dilo Makes Friends*. Writing continued as I flew across the Atlantic Ocean to Santa Fe in New Mexico. There I set off on a lecture tour with Rebecca Fitzgerald and her friend Bethanne, who took along her dog for company. Our car journey took us through deserts up into the snow-covered Rocky Mountains of Colorado and down to the beaches of California.

The aim of our expedition was to recruit clients for Rebecca's Dolphinswim programmes. Little did I know at the time that I would later join Rebecca on the tiny island of Bimini in the Bahamas where *Dilo Makes Friends* would be used for English lessons in a classroom that looked out directly onto a beach of coral sand, beyond which dolphins frolicked in a sun-dappled sea.

Many friends have helped me to get *Dilo and the Witch of Black Rock* into print. My special thanks go to Sue and Kirsty at Redcliff Print & Design who have transcribed my often wobbly pencil scrawl into perfectly printed and paragraphed text. Those who read through the drafts include: Jane Prowse, Rebecca Parker, Yvonne Dumsday, Jackie Connell, Adele Powell, Kris Simpson, Sonja Sitton, her daughter Ellie and many more. I thank them all for their much needed corrections and suggestions. When they had finished reading the manuscript most of them asked, "What happens next to Dilo?". To which I usually replied, "I'm not sure." You see I do much of my writing on boats, trains and planes. However, as I have been travelling quite alot lately I can now inform them that more books are well underway. I also tell them that Dilo keeps pushing me into new research and adventures. So I am looking forward to seeing where Dilo, my mischievous, make-believe dolphin, will lead me next. If you would like to follow my progress you can do so on the International Dolphin Watch website: www.idw.org

Indepth Horace